A Giant First-Start Reader

This easy reader contains only 38 different words, repeated often to help the young reader develop word recognition and interest in reading.

Basic word list for *Surprise Party*

a	hide	quiet
at	hiding	ready
be	is	see
come	it	she
comes	it's	surprise
dark	Kate	surprised
did	late	tell
don't	let	the
eight	lights	to
everyone	must	turn
for	out	what
hear	party	when
here		you

Surprise Party

Written by Sharon Gordon

Illustrated by Susan Hall

Troll Associates

Library of Congress Cataloging in Publication Data

Gordon, Sharon.
  Surprise party.

  Summary: A surprise party is given for Kate.
  [1. Parties—Fiction] I. Hall, Susan. II. Title.
PZ7.G65936Su   [E]   81-4869
ISBN 0-89375-521-4   AACR2
ISBN 0-89375-522-2 (pbk.)

It's a surprise party!

Come to a surprise party.
It's a surprise party for Kate.

She must be surprised.

Don't tell Kate.

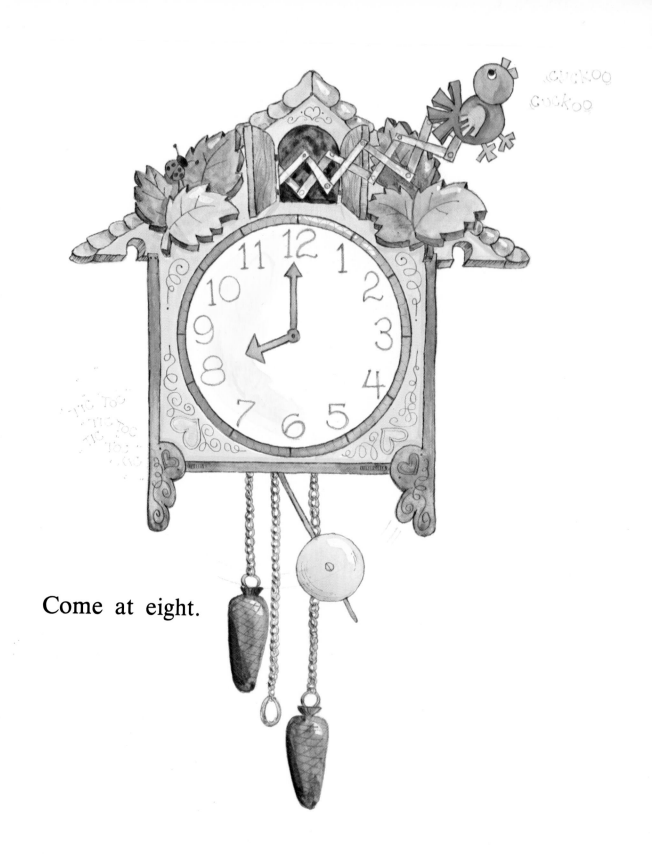

Come at eight.

Come to the surprise party at eight.

Don't be late.

Everyone must be quiet.

Don't let Kate hear you.

You must be quiet.

Everyone hide.

Don't let Kate see you.

She must be surprised.

Turn out the lights.

It must be dark.

It must be dark when Kate comes.

Is everyone ready?

Is everyone hiding?

Did you turn out the lights?

She must be surprised.

It's Kate!

Here comes Kate.

Ready? *Surprise!*

What a surprise!

What a surprise for Kate!